Catalina
and the
King's
Wall

Written by Patty Costello
Illustrated by Diane Cojocaru

Eifrig Publishing LLC
Berlin   Lemont

At Eifrig Publishing, our motto is our mission –
"Good for our kids, good for our Earth, and good for our communities.
We are passionate about helping kids develop into caring
creative, thoughtful individuals who possess positive self
images, celebrate differences, and practice inclusion. Ou
books promote social and environmental consciousness and
empower children as they grow in their communities
eifrigpublishing.com

Published by Eifrig Publishing,
PO Box 66, Lemont, PA 16851, USA
Knobelsdorffstr. 44, 14059 Berlin, Germany.

For information regarding permission, write to:
Rights and Permissions Department,
Eifrig Publishing,
PO Box 66, Lemont, PA 16851, USA.
permissions@eifrigpublishing.com,
+1-888-340-6543

Library of Congress Cataloging-in-Publication
Data

Costello, Patricia
Catlina and the King's Wall/
by Patricia Costello, illustrated by Diane Cojocaru

p. cm.

Paperback: ISBN 978-1-63233-101-4
Hardcover: ISBN 978-1-63233-105-2
Ebook: ISBN 978-1-63233-128-1

I. Cojocaru, Diane, ill. II. Title

[1. Inclusivity - Juvenile Fiction. 2. Diversity -
Juvenile Fiction.]

22 21 20 19 2018
5 4 3 2 1

Printed in the USA on acid-free paper with
recycled content. ∞

For Bjorn, my inspiration for this book
—P.C.

For Carol
—D.C.

In a not so faraway kingdom, not so long ago, there lived a girl named Catalina. Catalina created delicious delicacies for the king, but she really missed her family in the nearby kingdom.

Catalina hummed happily while she baked and buttered from the crack of dawn until the darkness of night. There was no time to visit her family in the nearby kingdom, but they were coming to see her soon.

One day Catalina brought the king her bite-sized cookies bursting with butterscotch. She overheard him say, "I do not like the people in the nearby kingdom. They are different. I must build a wall to keep them out!"

"Oh no," Catalina said to herself. "That means I'll never see my family. I've got to do something!" Catalina browned and blended while she plotted a plan.

Meanwhile, the king could not be pleased, not even in his playroom. "This cookie needs more chocolate! Where's my milk? I want marshmallows!" he bellowed.

"Oh boy," thought Catalina.
"He really frosts my cookies!"

Despite his ranting,
the king ate,

and **ate,**

and **ate**
her cookies.

The next time Catalina came with her crunchy crinkle cookies, she had a plan for the king, who clearly had no plan of his own. "I have something you can use to build your wall. It will be as easy as pie."

Catalina lugged over a giant vat of her brother's favorite icing. The king's workers built an ooey and gooey wall.

But soon the rain came. It rushed and gushed and the icing drooped, drizzled, and dripped all over the kingdom. Catalina smiled. She knew that would happen.

The king scowled. "Build me a new wall immediately!" he ordered his workers.

Catalina persisted. "I have something else you can use to build your wall!" She dragged over a wagon filled with her father's favorite sprinkles.

"A wall made of sprinkles?" the king asked suspiciously. "It will be a piece of cake!" replied Catalina. The workers built a spectacularly speckled wall.

But soon the wind began to blow. It growled and howled
and the sprinkles swirled, swooshed, and swished away.
Catalina smiled. She knew that would happen.

The king's face turned from orange to red. He demanded, "I need a wall that will last forever!"

"Oh, for goodness bakes!" Catalina said to herself.
"What shall I do?"
Catalina thought. And thought. Then her face lit up.
"I've got the recipe for success!"

She mixed a huge bowl of her mother's favorite cookie dough. "This is the cherry on top," she said to herself.

The king took some convincing, but finally agreed. The workers built a gigantic cookie dough wall. Catalina trembled with trepidation. "I hope this works!"

A fierce storm was brewing while the king inspected the new wall. "Finally, an indestructible wall!" he roared over the wind and rain.

Catalina frowned. She did not know THAT would happen.
"This wall is never going to fall down," Catalina cried.
She missed her family more than ever.

Inconceivable! A chunk of dough blew off and hit the king on the head.

Catalina had an idea. "Why don't you take a bit of a bite?" she slyly suggested.

The king took a nibble. His eyes lit up and a rare smile crossed his lips. "Mmmm, this wall is delicious!" he exclaimed. "I'll just take one more bite," he murmured. One bite led to another ... and another ... and another.

And the gluttonous king did not stop there. He kept eating and eating his own wall. Before long, only crumbs of cookie dough remained. The king clutched his belly. He could no longer move. A loud BURRRRRRP escaped his lips.

Catalina smiled. She knew that would happen.
"That's the way the cookie crumbles!"
Her family arrived right on time for their visit.
She gathered a fresh batch of her favorite cookies
and ran into their arms.

"Life sure is sweet," declared Catalina. And so it was, and so it is, and the king—too stuffed for his own good—never bothered anyone again.

Catalina's Cookies & Cakes

Menu

Cookies and Love

All are welcome here.

TODOS SON BIENVENIDOS AQUI

الجميع مرحب بهم هنا

CPSIA information can be obtained
at www.ICGtesting.com
Printed in the USA
LVHW07*1447080618
580105LV00022B/188/P